The Tree Stump

Roderick Hunt • Alex Brychta

OXFORD
UNIVERSITY PRESS

"That old stump has to go,"
said Dad.

Dad pulled the old stump,
but it didn't come up.

Dad called Mum to help.
"I'll push it. You pull it,"
said Dad.

"When I say pull," said Dad,
"I want you to pull!"

Mum pulled and pulled, but
the stump didn't come up.

Dad called Biff.

"I want you to pull," said Dad.

Mum and Biff pulled...
but the stump still didn't come up.

Dad wanted Chip to help.

"When I shout pull," said Dad,

"I want you to pull."

They all pulled...
but the stump still didn't come up.

Kipper wanted to help.

"Come on, then," said Dad.

"When I shout pull... PULL!"

They pulled and they pulled...
but the stump still didn't come up.

"I'll pull as well," said Dad.

"When I yell pull... PULL!"

They all pulled and pulled...
but the stump still didn't come up.

Floppy saw a bone.

He dug and he dug, and...

up came the stump!

BUMP!

"Good old Floppy!" said Chip.

Think about the story

Rhyming odd one out

Which things don't rhyme with snail?

Useful common words repeated in this story and other books at Level 3.

but   come   didn't   help   it   pull   they   up   want

Names in this story: Mum   Dad   Biff   Chip   Kipper   Floppy